This book belongs to

_____

_____

For all the children at Treewise
C.F.

Library of Congress Cataloging-in-Publication Data Available

1 2 3 4 5 6 7 8 9 10

Published in 2008 by Sterling Publishing Co., Inc.
387 Park Avenue South, New York, NY 10016

First published in Great Britain in 2008 by Gullane Children's Books
185 Fleet Street, London, EX4A 2HS
www.gullanebooks.com

Distributed in Canada by Sterling Publishing
c/o Canadian Manda Group
165 Dufferin Street, Toronto, Ontario, Canada M6K 3H6

Text and Illustrations copyright © 2008 Charles Fuge

Sterling ISBN 978-1-4027-6019-8

This is the Way

by Charles Fuge

STERLING

New York / London

This is the way the elephant walks

BOOM
BANG
CRASH!

And this is the way the dinosaur stalks

SNARL
HISS
GNASH!

This is the way the house mouse scurries

SKITTLE SKATTLE SKUTTLE!

And this is the way the ladybug hurries

BEETLE
BATTLE
BUTTLE!

This is the way the anteater creeps

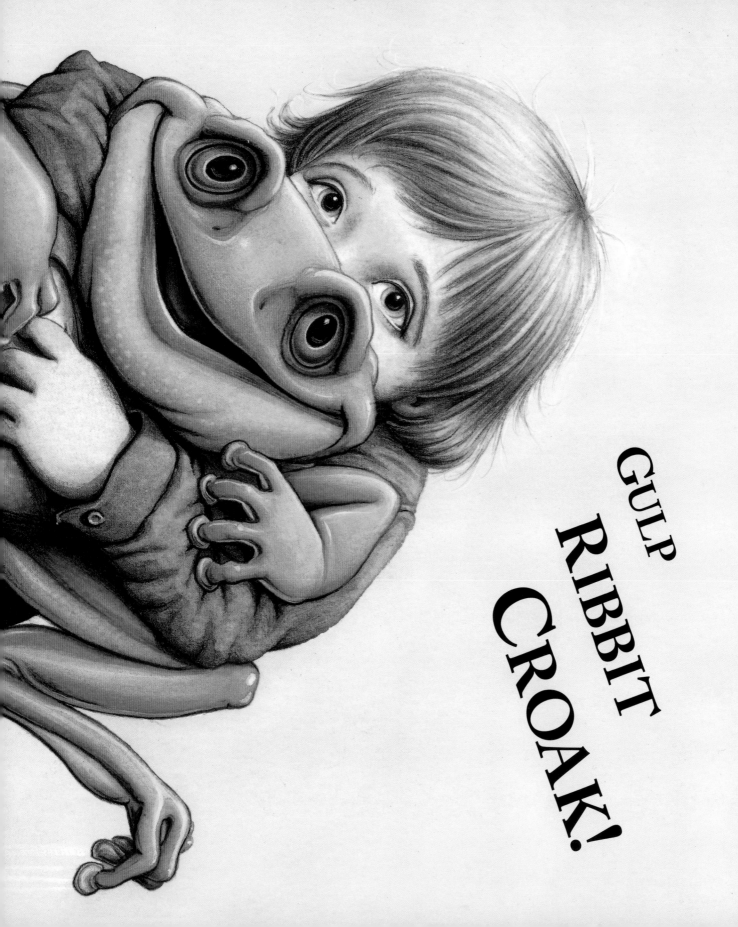

And this is the way the tree frog leaps

GULP
RIBBIT
CROAK!

This is the way
the orangutan swings

And this is the way
the owl sings

TAWIT
TAWIT
TAWOO!

This is the way
the bumble bee flies

BZZZ BZZZ BZZZ!

And these are my dreams when I close my eyes

ZZZZ   ZZZZ   ZZZZ!